J 567580
529 11.95
Hou

Hours, days, and years

DATE DUE			

GREAT RIVER REGIONAL LIBRARY
St. Cloud, Minnesota 56301

Ripley's — Believe It or Not!®

Mind Teasers

HOURS, DAYS AND YEARS

Published by
Capstone Press, Inc.
Mankato, Minnesota USA

567580

CIP
LIBRARY OF CONGRESS CATALOGING IN PUBLICATION DATA

Hours, days, and years.
    p. cm. -- (Ripley's believe it or not! mind teasers)
    Summary: Presents surprising facts about time, clocks, and calendars.

ISBN 1-56065-065-6:
1. Time--Juvenile literature. 2. Clocks and watches--Juvenile literature. 3. Calendars--Juvenile literature. 4. Curiosities and wonders--Juvenile literature. [1. Time--Miscellanea. 2. Clocks and watches--Miscellanea. 3. Calendars--Miscellanea. 4. Curiosities and wonders.] I. Series.
QB209.5.H84   1991
529--dc20   91-20638
                                CIP
                                AC

Color Illustrations by Carol J. Stott

Copyright ©1991 by Ripley Entertainment, Inc. All rights reserved. No part of this book may be used or reproduced in any manner whatsoever without written permission except in the case of reprints in the context of reviews. For information write Ripley's Believe it or Not! 90 Eglinton Ave. East, Suite 510, Toronto, Ontario, M4P 2Y3.

This edition published by Capstone Press, Inc., Box 669, Mankato, MN 56001. Printed in the United States of America.

CAPSTONE PRESS
Box 669, Mankato, MN 56001

Ripley's Believe It or Not!

CONTENTS

Introduction	5
Days	7
Hours	10
Years	35
Believe It or Not!	42

Introduction

The man that created Ripley's Believe It or Not! was Robert L. Ripley. Ripley grew up in Santa Rosa, California. His two main interests throughout his youth were drawing and sports. By the time he was 25, Ripley was working in New York for the Globe as a sports illustrator.

One day, when Ripley needed to fill space in the newspaper, he found a scrapbook with unusual achievements in sports in his files. He drew illustrations for 9 of these and titled the art "Champs and Chumps." Ripley's editor retitled the work "Believe It or Not!" This was published on December 19, 1918. The column was so popular that "Believe It or Not!" was set up as a regular weekly column. It was not long before it was a daily cartoon.

In 1929, Ripley was one of the top cartoonists in the country. His Believe It or Not! feature was one of the hottest columns in the newspaper. He had also published a book and was now anxious to search for new material. For the next few years he traveled thousands of miles. He visited 198 different countries. At first he returned with many souvenirs of personal interest. Soon, he started returning with huge crates of curiosities. His friends encouraged him to put his treasures on public display.

Ripley's first display was in 1933 at Chicago's Century of Progress Exposition. In two seasons 2,470,739 people lined up to see his incredible treasures. Now Ripley was in demand on the lecture circuit. Next came movies, a top-rated radio show, more books and finally television. By 1940, Ripley had three "Odditoriums" running simultaneously - one at the Golden Gate International Exposition in San Francisco, California; one at the World's Fair at Flushing Meadows, New York; and another on Broadway in New York City. A number of trailer shows toured the country. Ripley was very famous by the time of his death in 1949.

The information included in this special Mind Teaser Edition is from original Ripley's Believe It or Not! amazing archives of cartoons.

Ripley's Believe It or Not!

Days

THE 2 CHIMNEYS ON THE POORHOUSE OF ETWALL, ENGLAND, REVEAL THE TIME OF DAY **BY LARGE SUNDIALS**

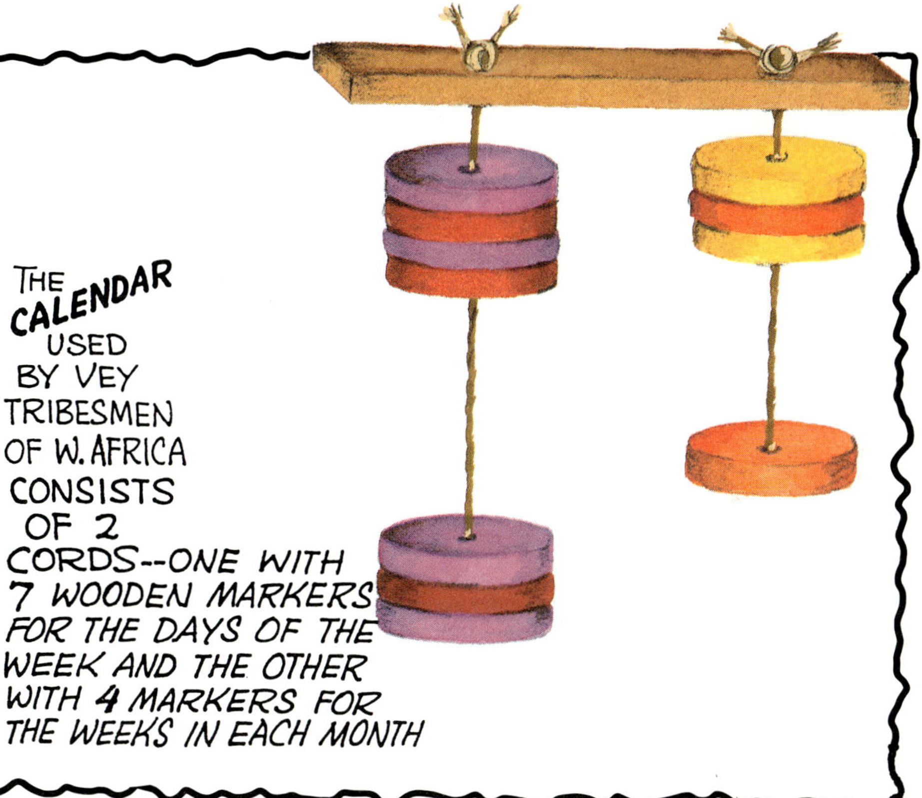

THE **CALENDAR** USED BY VEY TRIBESMEN OF W. AFRICA CONSISTS OF 2 CORDS--ONE WITH 7 WOODEN MARKERS FOR THE DAYS OF THE WEEK AND THE OTHER WITH 4 MARKERS FOR THE WEEKS IN EACH MONTH

Ripley's Believe It or Not!

Hours

THE GREAT CLOCK ON THE OLD CITY HALL of Prague, Czechoslovakia, HAS BEEN RUNNING WITHOUT PAUSE SINCE 1490 — *ITS PERPETUAL CALENDAR AND ANIMATED FIGURES BEING CONSIDERED A WONDER OF THE AGES* — YET IT HAS NOT ONCE SHOWN THE CORRECT TIME IN 478 YEARS

ELECTRONIC DIGITAL WATCHES CONTAIN A SMALL SLICE OF QUARTZ CRYSTAL THAT VIBRATES OVER **56,000** TIMES PER SECOND

THE PUBLIC CLOCK in the Borghese Park, Rome, Italy, *IS RUN SOLELY ON WATER POWER*

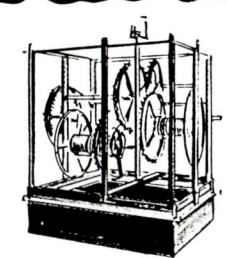

THE CLOCK INSTALLED IN SALISBURY CATHEDRAL, ENGLAND, IN 1386, WHICH SOUNDED THE HOURS BUT NEVER HAD A DIAL, IS THE *OLDEST CLOCK IN THE WORLD*

A NEW WATCH THAT CAN BE POWERED BY BEER, WATER, MILK, TEA, ORANGE JUICE, SODA OR ANY LIQUID, MUST BE DUNKED EVERY FEW DAYS

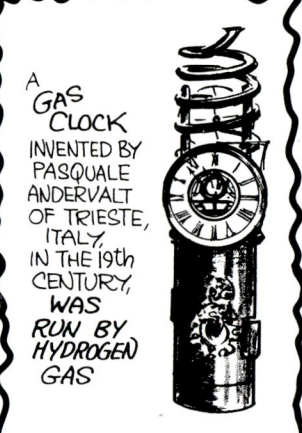

A **GAS CLOCK** INVENTED BY PASQUALE ANDERVALT OF TRIESTE, ITALY, IN THE 19th CENTURY, **WAS RUN BY HYDROGEN GAS**

A HUGE WRISTWATCH HUNG FROM A 37-STORY BUILDING IN TOKYO, JAPAN, IS 37 FEET LONG AND WEIGHS **12,000 POUNDS**

A **WRISTWATCH** OFFERED FOR SALE IN N.Y. CITY WITH A PRICE TAG OF $9,000 *IS AS THIN AS A CREDIT CARD*

12

AN ANCIENT CHINESE "CLOCK"

marked the hours by means of an incense stick, which as it burned severed strings holding metal discs placed at set intervals — the noise of their falling indicating the passage of a period of time

AN ALARM CLOCK
INVENTED IN 1500, SOUNDED THE HOUR — AND ALSO LIT A CANDLE

A SWISS WATCHMAKER HAS DESIGNED A CUCKOO WRIST WATCH WITH AN ALPINE CHALET, PINE CONES *AND A CUCKOO BIRD THAT POPS OUT EVERY HOUR!*

BRAUN, APPLIANCE COMPANY IN GERMANY, HAS DESIGNED A VOICE-ACTIVATED ALARM CLOCK THAT CAN ONLY BE SHUT OFF BY SHOUTING AT IT.

THE CLOCKS ON THE CHURCH AT MOSTA, MALTA, WERE SET AT DIFFERENT TIMES *TO CONFUSE THE DEVIL*

An **ALARM CLOCK** created in England in 1600, AWAKENED ITS OWNER BY *FIRING A BLANK CARTRIDGE*

THE WORLD'S LARGEST CLOCK WITH 4 FACES ON THE ALLEN-BRADLEY BUILDING IN MILWAUKEE, WIS., HAS A DIAMETER OF 40 FT., 3½ IN. ON EACH FACE WITH 20-FT.-LONG MINUTE HANDS WHOSE TIPS MOVE 125 FEET PER HOUR

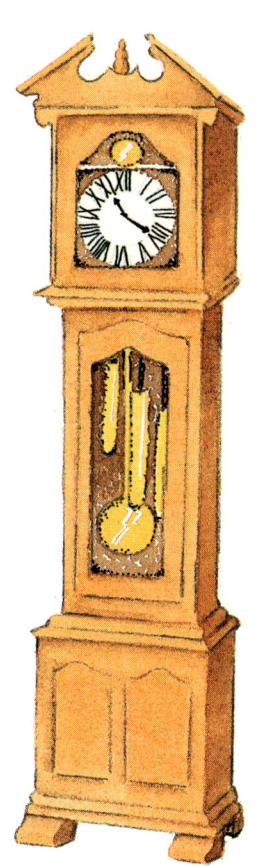

15

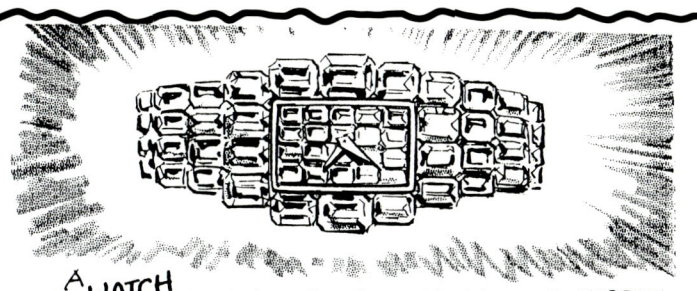

A **WATCH** DESIGNED BY PAINTER RAYMOND MORETTI IN PARIS, FRANCE, AND STUDDED WITH 130 CARATS OF DIAMONDS -- *IS PRICED AT OVER $3,500,000*

A **WATCH** OWNED BY MARY QUEEN OF SCOTS, MADE IN THE SHAPE OF A *HUMAN SKULL*

"TIME IS MONEY"

The Mastyn Tompion clock made in the late 1600s by Thomas Tompion for England's King William III is still accurate within seconds and requires winding only once a year... It was sold to The British Museum in 1982 for **$861,750**

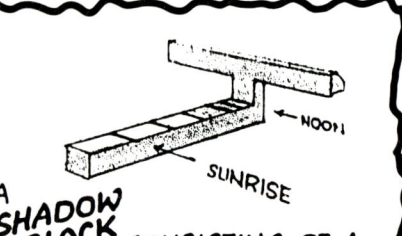

A **SHADOW CLOCK** CONSISTING OF A SHORT PIECE OF WOOD POINTING EASTWARD, WHICH CAST ITS SHADOW ON A LONGER BOARD ON WHICH WERE MARKED OFF THE HOURS FROM SUNRISE TO NOON—*USED IN EGYPT 3,400 YEARS AGO.*

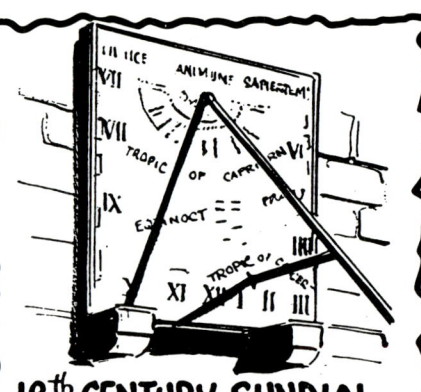

18th CENTURY SUNDIAL Eyam, England, TELLS TIME *THROUGHOUT THE WORLD*

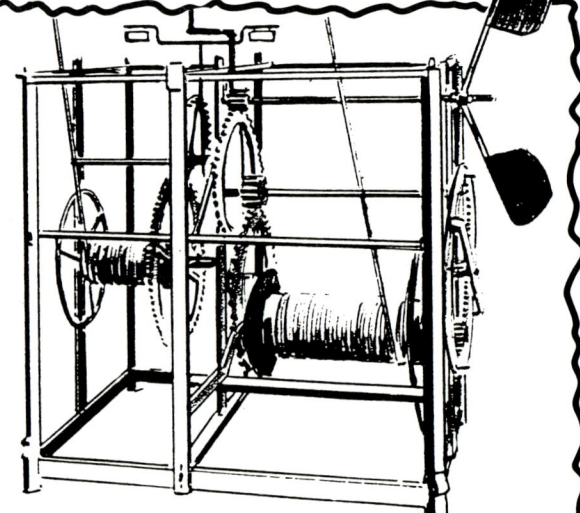

THE MEDIEVAL CLOCK OF SALISBURY CATHEDRAL IN ENGLAND, MADE ABOUT 1386, IS THE OLDEST EXISTING IN ENGLAND AND THE EARLIEST REMAINING MECHANICAL ONE IN WORKING CONDITION IN THE WORLD. IT HAS TICKED OVER 500,000,000 TIMES

IF — IT TAKES A CLOCK 6 SECONDS TO STRIKE 6 —
IT WILL TAKE THE SAME CLOCK 12 SEC. TO STRIKE 11

WHY?

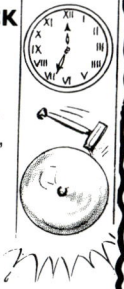

THE FIRST ALARM CLOCK making use of a bell was invented by Levi Hutchins of Concord, N.H., in 1787 but he wasn't wide awake enough to **PATENT IT**

RISE AND SHINE!
"FUDGE," A DOG IN ENGLAND, SWALLOWED A MUSICAL ALARM WATCH AND UNTIL HIS SUCCESSFUL OPERATION, TRILLED OUT A TUNE EACH MORNING AT 6:45

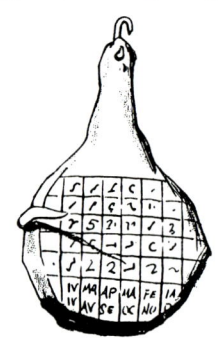

SUNDIALS
USED AS TIMEPIECES BY BUTCHERS IN MEDIEVAL EUROPE *WERE SHAPED LIKE A SIDE OF BEEF*

Each pair of opposite numbers on a pocket watch **ADDS UP TO 12**

The **MOST ACCURATE TIME MACHINE IN THE UNIVERSE**
IT IS EVEN MORE ACCURATE THAN THE MOVEMENT OF THE EARTH

Invented by
DR. HAROLD LYONS
National Bureau of Standards
Washington, D.C.

4 MEDIEVAL HOUR GLASSES BOUND TOGETHER AND FILLED WITH DIFFERENT AMOUNTS OF SAND *MEASURED 60 MINUTES, 45 MINUTES, 30 MINUTES AND 15 MINUTES*

A HUGE CUCKOO CLOCK LOCATED AT ALPINE-ALPA, WILMOT, OHIO, TOOK **12** YEARS TO BUILD (1962-74) AND IS 23½ FEET HIGH, **24** FEET LONG AND 13½ FEET WIDE

A SWISS WATCH COSTING OVER $30,000 *THAT IS ONLY 1.89 MILLIMETERS THICK*

ONE FACE OF A CLOCK IN THE TOWER OF THE CHURCH OF ST. GEORGE IN SOUTHWARK, LONDON, ENGLAND, IS BLACK AND HARD TO READ BECAUSE THE AREA FROM WHICH IT IS VISIBLE REFUSED TO CONTRIBUTE TO THE COST WHEN THE CLOCK WAS ERECTED **2 AND A HALF CENTURIES AGO**

BENJAMIN BANNEKER (1731-1806) WHO WAS BORN NEAR BALTIMORE, MD., *MADE THE FIRST WOODEN CLOCK IN AMERICA IN 1761, ALTHOUGH HE HAD NEVER SEEN A CLOCK*

A **TAX** ON CLOCKS INTRODUCED IN ENGLAND BY PRIME MINISTER WILLIAM PITT THE YOUNGER IN 1797, PROVED SO DISASTROUS THAT IT WAS REPEALED *THE VERY NEXT YEAR*

A **WRISTWATCH** WAS OFFICIALLY NOTED FOR THE FIRST TIME IN GENEVA, SWITZERLAND, IN 1790 AS "*A WATCH TO BE FIXED AS A BRACELET*"

The GONG BOYS of INDIA
A WATER CLOCK USED IN ANCIENT INDIA CONSISTED OF A LARGE VESSEL OF WATER IN WHICH WAS PLACED A BRONZE DISH WITH A HOLE IN ITS BOTTOM... A BOY SAT BESIDE THE WATER CLOCK AND WHEN THE INNER DISH SANK HE EMPTIED IT, STRUCK IT LIKE A GONG AND THEN REPLACED IT IN THE WATER

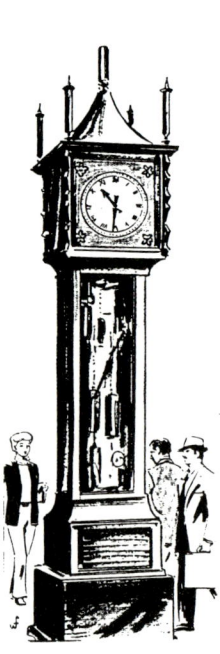

"PAGING RUBE GOLDBERG"

A HUGE SIDEWALK CLOCK IN Vancouver, B.C., with glass sides that show a conglomeration of chains lifting steel balls which roll down chutes, tripping levers that operate gears — toots the hours and keeps correct time **ENTIRELY BY STEAM POWER**

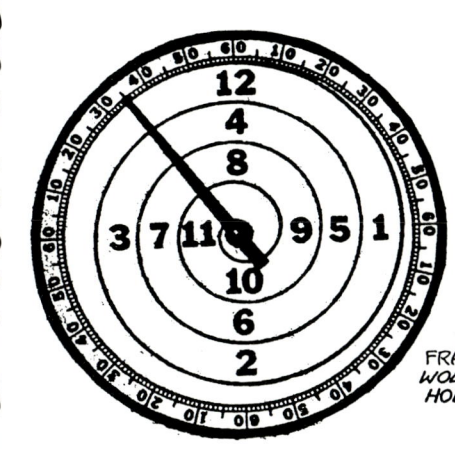

A Clock that gave you three guesses
A one-hand clock invented by Benjamin Franklin in 1770, *was not marketed until 200 years later*... The hand here reads either 3:35, 7:35 or 11:35, but Franklin figured anyone *would know about what hour of the day it was*

A **Silver Watch** buried in the earthquake of 1692 at Port Royal, Jamaica, was unearthed 275 years later... and restored to perfect working condition

Time Out!
A wristwatch lost by John Bembers, while fishing in Lake Michigan in 1976, was found by Thomas Kresnak of Grand Rapids, Mich., in the stomach of a 42-lb. salmon he caught in 1979

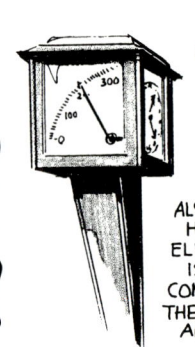

A **CLOCK** ON THE MAIN STREET OF ERLANGEN, GERMANY, TELLS THE TIME AND ALSO REVEALS HOW MUCH ELECTRICITY IS BEING CONSUMED IN THE TOWN AT ANY GIVEN MOMENT

"EVERYONE'S TIME" A HUGE WORK OF ART BY FRENCH SCULPTOR ARMAN IN THE SAINT-LAZARE R.R. STATION IN PARIS, IS A MONUMENT TO THE PROMPTNESS OF FRANCE'S RAIL TRANSPORT AND A COMMENT ON THE DOMINATION OF A BIG CITY **BY TIME**

GEORGE DANIELS of London, England, MAKES WATCHES ENTIRELY BY HAND -- TAKING AS LONG AS 3 YEARS TO BUILD ONE AND CHARGING A MINIMUM OF $16,000 EACH

A TIME BALL
WHICH DROPPED EXACTLY AT NOON, WAS USED IN MANY CITIES BEFORE THE DAYS OF RADIO TO *ENABLE CITIZENS TO SET THEIR WATCHES*

THOMAS WILLIS PITTS
AN AMERICAN P.O.W., GAVE HIS WATCH TO A FELLOW PRISONER FOR BREAD AT A MUHLBERG PRISON CAMP IN 1945. 43 YEARS LATER, IN 1988, THEODORE WILLIAM YOUNG, RETURNED THE WATCH TO PITTS' WIDOW -- AND IT WAS STILL IN WORKING ORDER

AN **HOURGLASS** WAS STRAPPED ON THE KNEE OF FASHIONABLE YOUNG GERMANS IN THE 16th CENTURY -*AN ORNAMENTAL FORERUNNER OF THE MODERN WRIST WATCH*

THE "MARIE ANTOINETTE"
A MAGNIFICENT TIMEPIECE ORDERED IN 1783 AND NAMED AFTER FRANCE'S QUEEN WAS NEVER SEEN BY HER... IT WAS COMPLETED IN 1823, **30 YEARS AFTER HER EXECUTION!**
NO PRICE TAG OR COMPLETION DATE HAD EVER BEEN IMPOSED

SPHERICAL CLOCKS IN 17th-CENTURY GERMANY WERE SUSPENDED FROM CHAINS WHICH REWOUND THEM AS THE CLOCKS SLIPPED DOWN

THE WORLD'S MOST COMPLICATED WATCH, THE CALIBRE 89, *HAS 1728 PARTS AND TOOK 9 YEARS TO BUILD.* MADE BY THE SWISS COMPANY PATEK PHILIPPE, *THE TIMEPIECE IS WORTH $6,000,000!*

A **COMPUTERIZED CLOCK** INVENTED BY AHMED BAHGAT FATTOUH, AN ENGINEER BORN IN EGYPT, TELLS MOSLEMS WHEN IT IS TIME FOR ONE OF THEIR FIVE PRAYERS A DAY PLUS THE DIRECTION OF MECCA IN WHICH THEY MUST FACE

THE ORIGINAL MINUTE MAN!
ALI ABUL HASSAN of Cairo, Egypt, A 13th-CENTURY ASTRONOMER, DIVIDED THE EQUINOX-- THE TIME WHEN DAY AND NIGHT ARE THE SAME LENGTH-- INTO **12** EQUAL PARTS *AND THUS ESTABLISHED THE HOUR OF 60 MINUTES* - PREVIOUSLY THE LENGTH OF THE HOUR HAD VARIED WITH THE SEASONS FOR 7,000 YEARS

CHINESE WATER CLOCK ON WHICH 3 SPOONS, IN CYCLES OF ONLY 2 HOURS, *DIP TO INDICATE TIME*

THE CLOCK ON THE CITY HALL OF ORANGE, FRANCE, AFTER STRIKING 5 O'CLOCK EACH AFTERNOON, SOUNDS AN ALARM TO NOTIFY THE CITIZENRY *IT IS TIME TO WASH THE STREET IN FRONT OF THEIR HOMES*

STEVE MILIN, A JEWELER IN CHICAGO, ILL., SELLS *"DISTRESS WATCHES"* — TIMEPIECES *THAT HAVE BEEN SMASHED AND BROKEN* — FOR $200.!

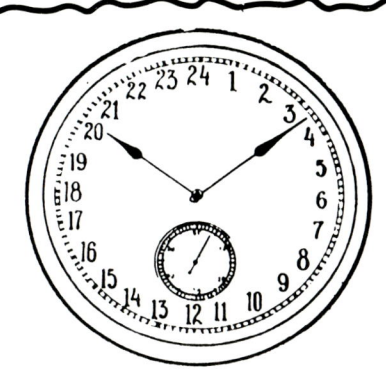

A **WATCH DIAL** EMPLOYED BY THE U.S. MILITARY AND SOME EUROPEANS, COVERED ALL 24 HOURS IN A DAY

1880's CLOCK WATCHERS SET THEIR WATCHES TO LOCAL STANDARD TIMES.. **WISCONSIN ALONE HAD 38 DIFFERING TIME ZONES!** UNIFORM STANDARDS WERE NOT ADHERED TO UNTIL MODERN TRANSPORTATION, INDUSTRY AND COMMUNICATIONS MADE THEM NECESSARY

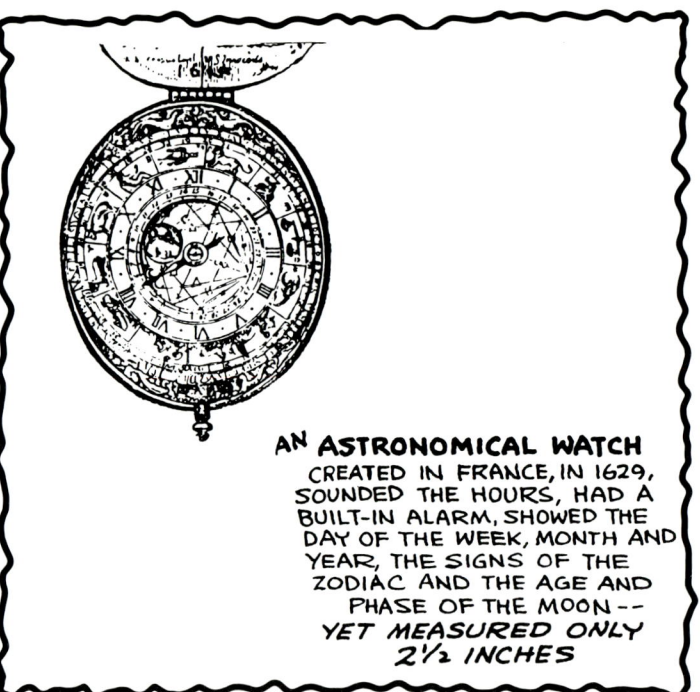

AN ASTRONOMICAL WATCH
CREATED IN FRANCE, IN 1629, SOUNDED THE HOURS, HAD A BUILT-IN ALARM, SHOWED THE DAY OF THE WEEK, MONTH AND YEAR, THE SIGNS OF THE ZODIAC AND THE AGE AND PHASE OF THE MOON -- *YET MEASURED ONLY 2½ INCHES*

THE OLYMPIC STADIUM in Helsinki, Finland, *IS A HUGE SUNDIAL*
SPORT FANS CAN ALWAYS TELL THE TIME BY THE SHADOW OF THE STADIUM TOWER

A LAMP CLOCK OF THE 1800s, CONTAINED OIL IN ITS GLASS GLOBE AND AS IT BURNED THE *HOUR WAS RECORDED ON A METAL BAND*

AN **ASTRONOMICAL CLOCK** INVENTED AT K'AI FENG, CHINA, IN THE 11th CENTURY, WAS THE BREAKTHROUGH BETWEEN PRIMITIVE WATER CLOCKS AND SPRING-DRIVEN TIMEPIECES BECAUSE IT HAD *ADJUSTABLE WEIGHTS*

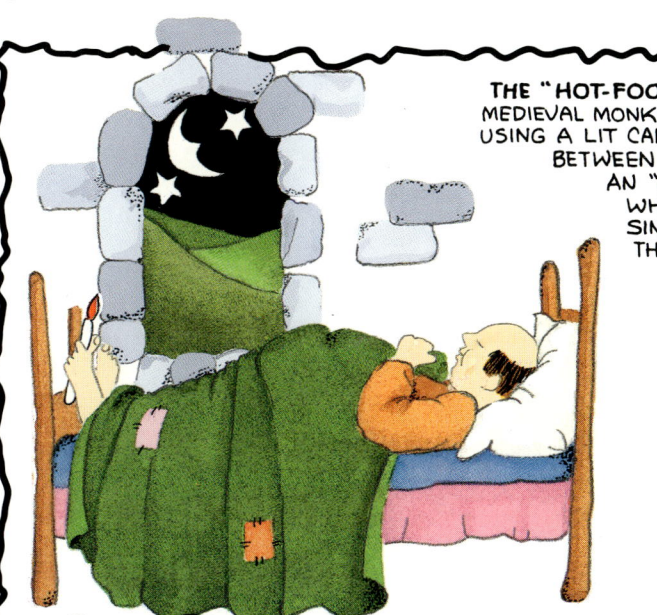

THE "HOT-FOOT CLOCK" MEDIEVAL MONKS AWOKE BY USING A LIT CANDLE PLACED BETWEEN THEIR TOES AS AN "ALARM CLOCK." WHEN THE FLAME SINGED THEIR SKIN, THEY KNEW IT WAS TIME TO RISE AND SHINE

2-FACED CLOCK WITH A SECOND HAND IN A SEPARATE DIAL, WAS INVENTED IN 1758 **BY BENJAMIN FRANKLIN**

THE CLOCKS ON THE CHURCH AT MOSTA, MALTA, WERE SET AT DIFFERENT TIMES *TO CONFUSE THE DEVIL*

A **CLOCK** MADE In England in 1691, DIVIDED THE DAY AND NIGHT **INTO 10 HOURS EACH**

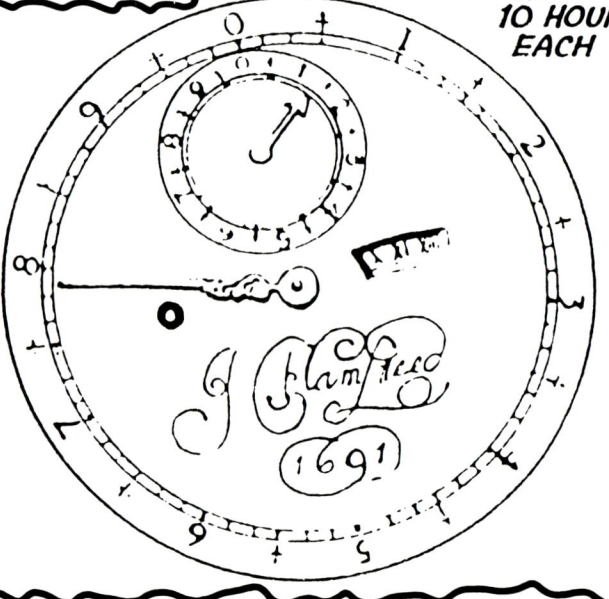

Ripley's Believe It or Not!

Years

THE MAN WHO GAVE THE WORLD THE CALENDAR

CNEIUS FLAVIUS a Roman IN 304 B.C. *BECAME THE FIRST MAN TO PUBLISH A CALENDAR*

BEFORE THAT TIME CALENDARS WERE THE SECRET POSSESSIONS OF PUBLIC OFFICIALS — WHO MANIPULATED THEIR CONTENTS AT WILL

THE **GREGORIAN CALENDAR** IS SO CLOSELY TIMED TO THE EARTH'S SOLAR ORBIT *THAT IT VARIES LESS THAN A DAY IN 3,000 YEARS*

CHINESE CALENDAR which dates back to the 27th century B.C. has associated with it **FIVE ELEMENTS AND 12 ANIMALS**

TURTLES IN PAPUA, NEW GUINEA, COME ASHORE EVERY DECEMBER TO LAY THEIR EGGS. THE AEK-YOM PEOPLE COUNT THE YEARS AND THEIR AGES BY **THE TIMES THE TURTLES LEAVE THE SEA FOR THE LAND**

A **CALENDAR WHEEL** used by the ancient Aztecs of Mexico TRACED THE INTRICATE ORBITS OF THE EARTH AND MOON AND ACCURATELY FORECAST ECLIPSES

An **AZTEC STONE CALENDAR** AT THE PYRAMID OF THE SUN IN MEXICO CITY, MEXICO, WEIGHS 20 TONS AND COVERS THE ENTIRE HISTORY OF THE WORLD TO THE 12th CENTURY

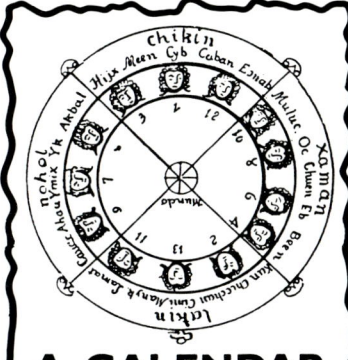

A CALENDAR of the ancient Maya Indians of Mexico was a wheel based on a year of **13 MONTHS**

ELIZABETH H. CULLEN BORN FEB. 30, 1760 RELICT OF CHARLES M. CULLEN DEPARTED THIS LIFE SEPT. 30, 1838

EPITAPH OF A WOMAN *BORN ON A DATE THAT NEVER WAS!* St. Peter's Churchyard Lewes, Delaware

37

GEORGE WASHINGTON LOST HIS 21ST BIRTHDAY

HE WOULD HAVE BEEN 21 ON FEB. 22, 1752 -- BUT THE CALENDAR WAS CHANGED AT THAT TIME *AND THERE WAS NO FEBRUARY IN 1752*

THE **CALENDAR** OF THE MAYAS OF MEXICO INCLUDED A UNIT KNOWN AS THE ALAUTUN, WHICH COMPRISED 23,040,000,000 DAYS -- *EQUIVALENT TO 64 MILLION YEARS*

FRIDAY THE 13TH CAN COME NO MORE THAN THREE TIMES IN ANY ONE YEAR AS IT DID IN 1987 -- BUT THE GOOD NEWS FOR THE SUPERSTITIOUS IS THAT BAD LUCK'S NEXT TRIPLE THREAT IS NOT DUE AGAIN UNTIL 1998

THE TONALAMATL
A HOROSCOPE 20 FEET IN LENGTH WAS CONSULTED BY AZTECS TO DETERMINE THE GOOD AND BAD DAYS FOR A NEWBORN BABY

THE FIRST OF THE MONTH
IN ANCIENT TIMES WAS OFFICIALLY PROCLAIMED BY A HEAD PRIEST AND NO ONE ELSE KNEW IN ADVANCE WHEN THE NEW MONTH WOULD START

THE **ROMAN LEAP YEAR** HAD ONE DAY — FEB. 23 — WHICH LASTED 48 HOURS

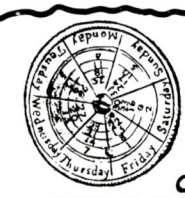

PERPETUAL POCKET CALENDARS MADE OF SILVER, WERE AVAILABLE IN EUROPE *IN THE 17th CENTURY*

THE 2-BIRTHDAY PEOPLE

ENGLISHMEN WHO WERE BORN ON FEB. 29TH, BY A STATUTE ORDERED BY KING HENRY VIII, CELEBRATED THEIR BIRTHDAYS IN NON-LEAP YEARS ON FEB. 28TH

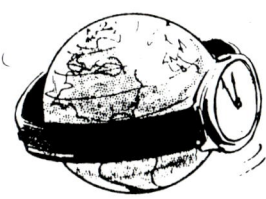

SCIENTISTS

since 1972, to match the world standard clocks to the spinning of the earth, have added one second to the old year

LEAP YEAR

WILL CEASE TO EXIST IN A FEW MILLION YEARS BECAUSE THE EARTH'S ROTATION RATE IS SLOWING AND *THERE WILL BE 365 DAYS IN THE YEAR INSTEAD OF TODAY'S 365.25*

Ripley's Believe It or Not!

THE MOST AMAZING TIME OF THIS CENTURY: AT 56 SECONDS AFTER 12:34 ON JULY 8, 1990, THIS PERFECT SEQUENCE WILL TELL THE TIME — 12:34:56, 7/8/90

IN 1656, IRISH ARCHBISHOP JAMES USSHER CALCULATED THAT THE EARTH WAS CREATED AT EXACTLY 8 P.M. ON SAT. OCT. 3, 4004, B.C.

THE ASTRONOMICAL CLOCK of the Cathedral of Beauvais, France
MADE IN **1866** - HAS **90,000** MOVING PARTS - **52** DIALS - **50** HUMAN FIGURES - **86** CONSTELLATIONS AND **4,000** STARS -- ALL THE STARS VISIBLE IN THE HEAVENS TO THE NAKED EYE

The **BACKWARD CLOCK** IT LOOKS LIKE A WATCH **AND RUNS COUNTER-CLOCKWISE**

THE FIRST CALENDAR WAS THE GREAT PYRAMID OF CHEOPS!
THE SHADOW CAST BY THE PYRAMID ENABLED THE EGYPTIANS TO DISCOVER THE RELATIONSHIP OF THE EARTH AND THE SUN, THE 4 SEASONS, AND OUR MODERN METHOD OF MEASURING TIME — *THE FIRST YEAR DETERMINED BY THIS CALENDAR WAS 4236 B.C.*

"TIME FLIES"

BELIEVE IT OR NOT! MORTON RACHOFSKY OF DALLAS, TEXAS, HAS INVENTED A CLOCK WITH 25 HOURS!

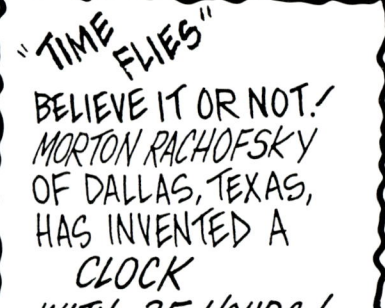

A CANDLE CLOCK POPULAR IN THE 19th CENTURY DROPPED METAL PELLETS AT REGULAR INTERVALS AS THE WAX CANDLE BURNED

PATENT #889,928
A PATENT FOR AN ALARM CLOCK THAT *SPRAYS WATER ON THE FACE OF A SLEEPING PERSON* WAS FILED AT THE U.S. PATENT OFFICE IN 1907!

A POCKET WATCH

BUILT FOR U.S. AUTO TYCOON JAMES PACKARD IN THE 1920s FOR $16,000 FETCHED $1,300,000 IN 1988. ITS DIALS SHOW MOON PHASES, SUNSETS AND SUNRISES AND EVEN LEAP YEARS. THE WATCH TOOK FIVE YEARS TO MAKE

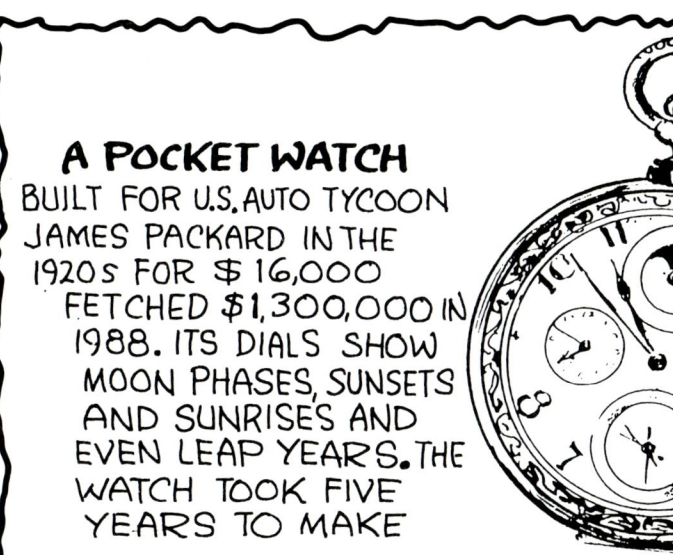

A $250,000 WATCH

DESIGNED BY SWISS WATCHMAKER MICHEL ROCHAT, TOOK AN EXTRA 3 MONTHS TO MAKE BECAUSE HE MISCALCULATED A PART'S POSITION BY 1/100th OF A MILLIMETER!

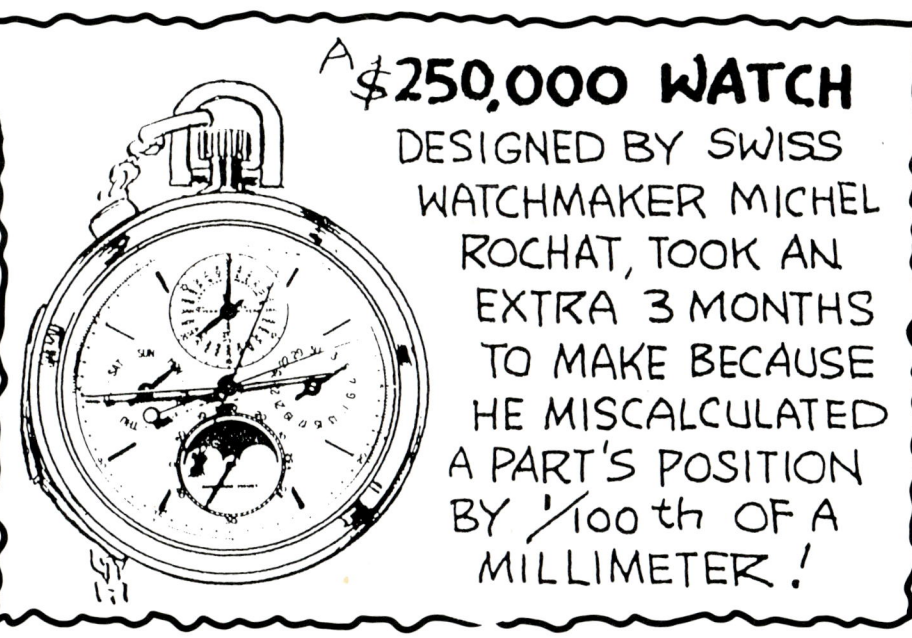

THE TURTLE CLOCK COMPRISES A MECHANICAL TURTLE FLOATING IN A BOWL OF WATER. MAGNETISM RIPPLES THE WATER, AND EVERY MINUTE THE TURTLE TOUCHES THE RIM OF THE BOWL *AT THE PROPER MARK INDICATING THE TIME OF THE DAY*

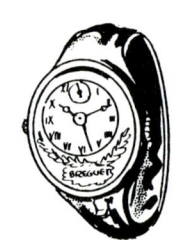

A CLOCK RING CREATED BY MASTER FRENCH WATCHMAKER BREGUET (1747-1823) HAD AS AN ALARM A PIN THAT STUCK THE WEARER'S FINGER AT THE TIME HE SET

PASSAGE OF TIME WAS NOTED IN ANCIENT TIMES, AT NIGHT WHEN SUNDIALS COULD NOT FUNCTION, BY BURNING LENGTHS OF ROPE *KNOTTED AT REGULAR INTERVALS*

SOSIGENES
an Egyptian astronomer
DIED OF A BROKEN HEART BECAUSE OF A CHANGE IN HIS INVENTION OF LEAP YEAR!

SOSIGENES CREATED THE JULIAN CALENDAR WITH AN EXTRA DAY EVERY 4 YEARS -- BUT IN 40 B.C. AUGUSTUS CAESAR INSISTED ON A LEAP YEAR EVERY 3 YEARS

THE WOMAN WHO WAS BURIED IN A CLOCK!
PAULA BESWICK OF SALE, ENGLAND, LEFT A FORTUNE TO HER PHYSICIAN -WITH THE STIPULATION THAT HE LOOK UPON HER FACE ONCE EACH YEAR AS LONG AS HE LIVED! HER EMBALMED BODY WAS KEPT IN THE CASE OF A GRANDFATHER'S CLOCK FOR 111 YEARS

January 1, 2000
WILL NOT BE THE FIRST DAY OF THE 21st CENTURY

The MOURNING CLOCK
THE ASTRONOMICAL CLOCK of Hampton Court, London, WHICH WAS CONSTRUCTED IN 1540, *HAS ALWAYS STOPPED WHEN ANY LONG-TIME RESIDENT OF THE PALACE DIES*

JANUARY
WAS CALLED WOLF MONTH BY THE ANCIENT SAXONS BECAUSE HUNGRY WOLVES INVADED THEIR VILLAGES AT THAT TIME AND ATTACKED PEOPLE!